ABC
I Like Me!

By Nancy Carlson

SCHOLASTIC INC.
New York   Toronto   London   Auckland   Sydney
Mexico City   New Delhi   Hong Kong

**This book is dedicated to
the memory of my Grandma Dorothy.
She was a *great* teller of jokes!**

ISBN 0-590-68036-6

25 24 23 22 21   6/0

Printed in the U.S.A.   40

First Scholastic printing, September 1998

Set in Publicity Gothic

Feeling good about me
is as easy as ABC!

I am **A**wesome,

Brave, and

Cheerful.

I have big Dreams,

and I like to Explore.

I am a good Friend.

I love to **Giggle**

and be Happy.

I have a great

Imagination.

I can Jump and Juggle.

I am **Kind.**

I am a good Leader.

Sometimes, I make Mistakes.

And sometimes, I'm Noisy!

I love to play **O**utside.

I try to be **P**olite.

I like **Quiet** times

so I can **Read.**

I am good at Sharing.

I am Talented!

Look at me—I'm Unique!

I try to eat all my Vegetables.

I like to make Wishes.

XXX OOO!

Yawn . . . I need a good

night's sleep, so tomorrow . . .

I can Zoom on!